other Time!

Written by **Nandini Ahuja**

Illustrated by **Catalina Echeverri**

HARPER FESTIVAL
An Imprint of HarperCollins Publishers

To my parents, who taught me how to write, read, love, and be a sister.

To my sisters, who love to play dress up, get me out of trouble,
and want me on their team.

To my husband, who tells the funniest jokes, builds the coziest pillow forts,
and always lets me hold the popcorn.
—N. A.

To Felix and his Big Sister, Emilia
—C. E.

HarperFestival is an imprint of HarperCollins Publishers.

It's Big Brother Time!

Library of Congress Control Number: 2019944046
ISBN 978-0-06-288437-4

Typography by Honee Jang
21 22 23 24 PC 10 9 8 7 6 5 4 3 2
❖
First Edition

Mom and Dad brought home someone new today.

"It's our baby," they say.

I ask Mom how long the baby
will be staying with us.
She says, "Forever!"

"Baby will be your new best friend."

I've never had a friend like *this*.

Baby's loud.

Baby's messy.

Sometimes Baby
really smells.

Maybe Baby doesn't know
the house rules yet.

I tell Dad that he should
probably have a talk with Baby.

But Dad says, "You'll have
to teach Baby the rules since
you're the big brother."

I guess I can help Baby
learn the rules.

After all, I was a baby too.
And I was *really* good at it.

Rule number one: There's absolutely no playing with my toys.

Even if you really want to

. . . unless I say so.

At nap time, you can't sleep with my
big boy blankie.

Even if it's just the right size for you.

When Grandma and Grandpa
come over to bake sweet potato pie,
I get to be their helper.

Even if you get the chef's hat.

You've got to put Mom's head wraps away before she gets home from work.

Even if you're in the middle of fighting crime.

There's no building pillow forts at bedtime,
especially after getting tucked in.

Even though pillow forts
are *really* cozy.

On movie night, I get to sit between
Mom and Dad and hold the popcorn.

But I guess I can hold you instead.

When my friends come over to play,
you have to be on my team.

Even if they ask nicely.

When it's time to sleep,
you have to be very quiet.

Even if someone tells a really funny joke.

If you accidentally make a mess,
you can ask me for help.

Even if it's a *big* mess.

The last and most important rule is,
no matter what, we stick together.

Because . . .

we're a team now.